Animal Supermarket

Written by
Giovanna Zoboli

Illustrated by
Simona Mulazzani

Translated by
Laura Watkinson

EERDMANS BOOKS FOR YOUNG READERS

GRAND RAPIDS, MICHIGAN • CAMBRIDGE, U.K.

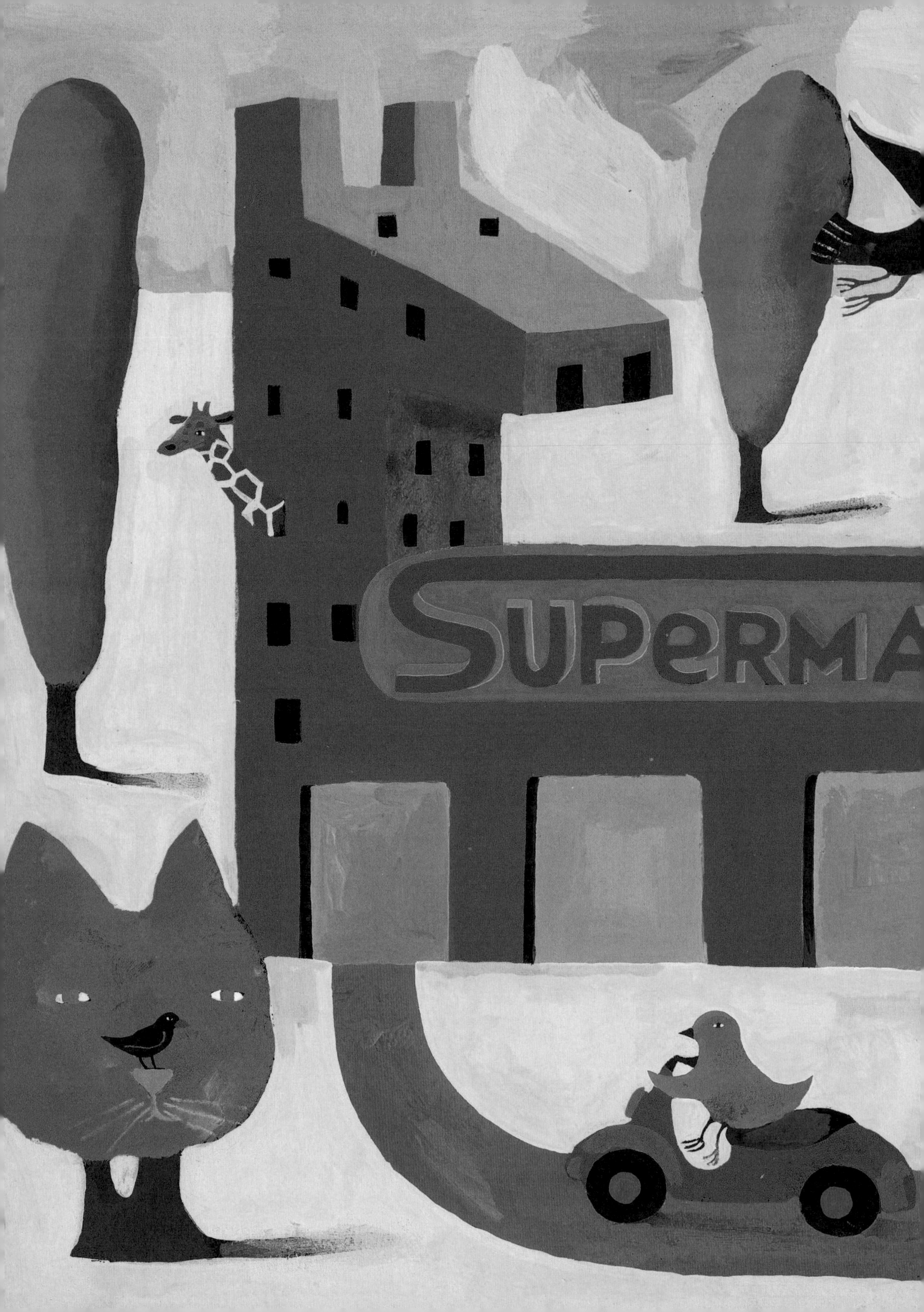
SUPERMA

The Animal Supermarket sells only natural foods. None of the customers want ice cream, cookies, or chips. There's no point looking for pizza or sugary snacks.

The snail is the first shopper this morning. She fills her cart with lettuce, kale, and herbs.

The elephants get family-size packs.
All those leaves won't fit inside their
trunks, so they haul them away in trucks.

Over in the produce aisle, two bears are picking out some blueberries. They'll eat them tonight at the cricket's concert.

What's that noise? A three-for-two sale
on crumbs? The birds twitter and the ants
form a long line. What a bargain!

The goat goes crazy for
turnips, gourds, and beets.
He shares a cart with the cow,
and they fill it right up.

You'll find the polar bears at the seafood
counter. What's on their shopping list?
Cod, cuttlefish, and squid.

Back in the fresh fruit aisle, more noisy birds chitter
and chatter. Apples? Pears? So much to choose from!
You'll never find the monkeys far from the bananas.
The cat is stocking up on milk — the kind with
the double cream.

The dog has found a tasty bone, but the toucan is still searching for termites. If they've run out of bamboo again, the panda will complain.

Who's that over by the checkout? It's the seals,
lining up with mackerel and cans of sardines.

The frozen food section was never very popular.
They closed it down last year and put in a
meadow instead.

The meadow is full of poppies, bluebells, and violets.
The bees carry their baskets from flower to flower.

There's a section for the lemurs and the gibbons, too, full of insects and grubs.

Rats and mice, of all colors and sizes,
climb on to the dairy counter to choose
the best cheese.

Up in the branches of the hazelnut tree, a sleepy dormouse reaches for some nuts. Down below, the twins help Mom Tapir shop for potatoes and tomatoes.

Look out! It's the fox and the mongoose. One snatches the chicken, while the other steals the eggs.

Just before closing time, the snail comes
back again, all out of breath.
"What bad luck!" she says. "How could
I forget the mushrooms for my salad?"

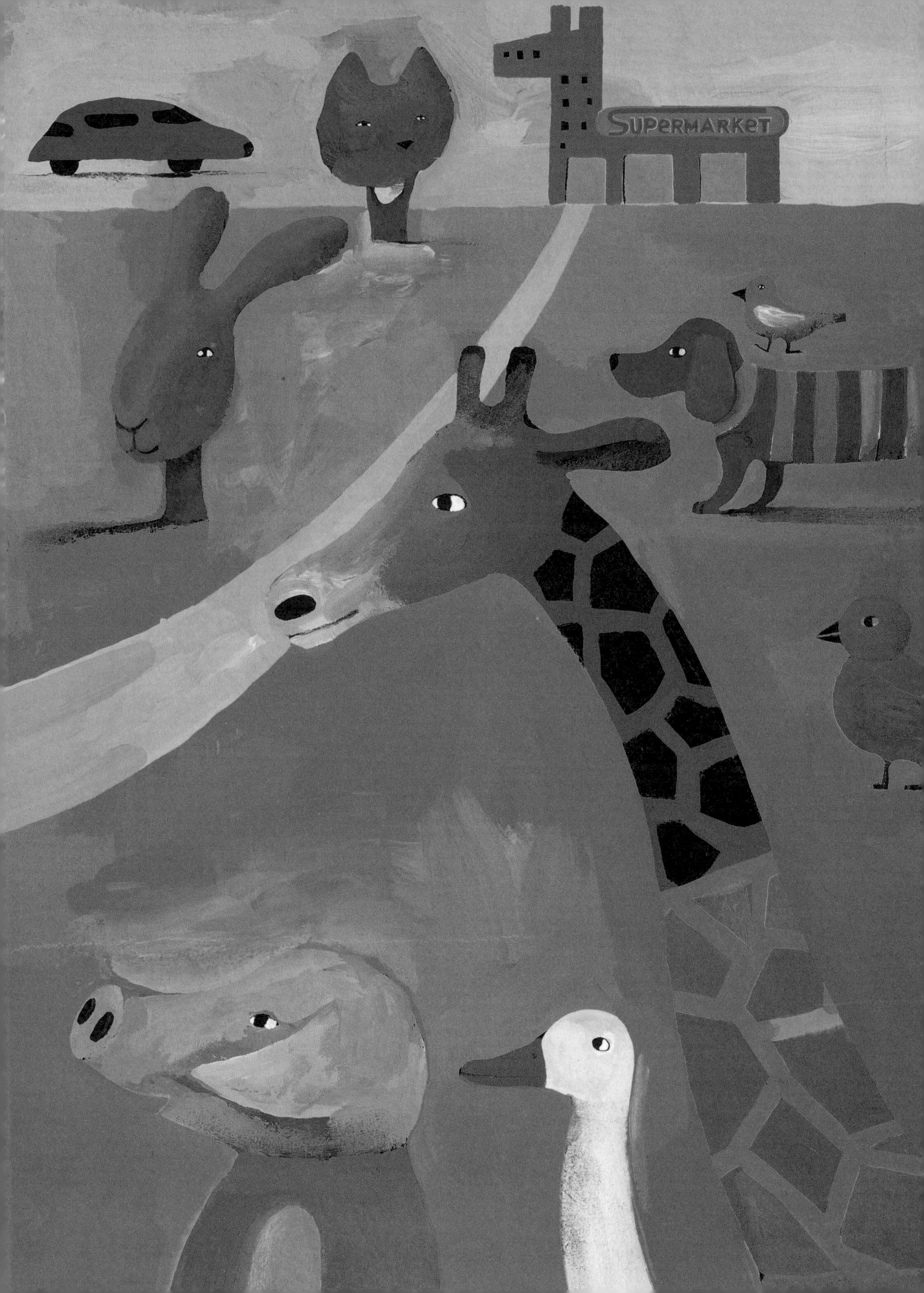
SUPERMARKET

What does each animal eat?

GIOVANNA ZOBOLI and **SIMONA MULAZZANI** have collaborated on several previous books, including *The Big Book of Slumber* and *I Wish I Had . . .* (both Eerdmans), which was awarded the Silver Medal in the Society of Illustrators' "The Original Art" Annual Exhibition. Both of them live in Italy.

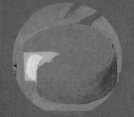

First published in the United States in 2015 by
Eerdmans Books for Young Readers,
an imprint of Wm. B. Eerdmans Publishing Co.
2140 Oak Industrial Dr. NE
Grand Rapids, Michigan 49505
P.O. Box 163, Cambridge CB3 9PU U.K.

www.eerdmans.com/youngreaders

Originally published in Italy in 2007 under the title
Al Supermercato degli Animali
by Topipittori, viale Isonzo 16, 20135 Milan, Italy
www.topipittori.it

Text © 2007 Giovanna Zoboli
Illustrations © 2007 Simona Mulazzani
© 2007 Topipittori, Milano
Translation © 2015 Laura Watkinson

Manufactured at Toppan Leefung in China

21 20 19 18 17 16 15   9 8 7 6 5 4 3 2 1

Library of Congress Cataloging-in-Publication Data

Zoboli, Giovanna.
[Al supermercato degli animali. English]
Animal Supermarket / by Giovanna Zoboli; illustrated by Simona
Mulazzani; translated by Laura Watkinson.
pages cm
Originally published in Italian by Topipittori in 2007 under title:
Al supermercato degli animali.
Summary: All kinds of species come to do their grocery shopping at
the Animal Supermarket — polar bears prowl the seafood section, cats
stock up on milk, and mice crowd the cheese counter.
ISBN 978-0-8028-5448-3
[1. Supermarkets — Fiction. 2. Grocery shopping — Fiction.
3. Animals — Food — Fiction.] I. Mulazzani, Simona, illustrator.
II. Watkinson, Laura, translator. III. Title.

PZ7.Z713An 2015
[E] — dc23

2014028079